ABDO Publishing Company is the exclusive school and library distributor of Rabbit Ears Books.

Library bound edition 2007.

Copyright © 1995 Rabbit Ears Entertainment, LLC.,
S. Norwalk, Connecticut.

Library of Congress Cataloging-in-Publication Data

Johnson, David, 1951 Feb. 18-
The boy who drew cats / retold & illustrated by David Johnson.
  p. cm.
Summary: An artistic boy's obsession with drawing cats leads him to a mysterious
experience. Based on a legend about the Japanese artist Sesshu Toyo.
ISBN-13: 978-1-59961-305-5
ISBN-10: 1-59961-305-0
1. Sesshu, 1420–1506—Legends. [1. Sesshu, 1420–1506—Legends. 2.
Folklore—Japan.] I. Title.

PZ8.1.J588Bo 2006
398.2095202—dc22

2006042594

All Rabbit Ears books are reinforced library binding
and manufactured in the United States of America.

ABDO
Publishing Company

THE BOY WHO DREW CATS

RETOLD & ILLUSTRATED
BY DAVID JOHNSON

RABBIT EARS BOOKS

I'm afraid I can't tell you the name of the village in which any of this took place. In fact I can't even tell you in which of Japan's sixty-six prefectures, or even in what year of the benevolent reign of which emperor any of this occurred. For all of this happened so very long ago that there isn't a soul alive who could possibly remember any of it.

Nonetheless, once upon a time, in Japan, there lived a farmer and his family. They were a large family, with many mouths to feed, but as everyone was willing to do whatever they could to help out, they lived a happy, although humble, life together.

Cne season, however, a terrible famine came to the village. All of the rice fields became dry and cracked; the gardens became choked with nettles and dock; the carefully tended fruit trees fell barren. It was the grim work of a hideous demon that had infested the countryside, where it became his evil pleasure to wreak havoc and destroy life.

Still, the farmer would go out every morning to glean what little rice the goblin had scattered and left, or to dig for such roots, and gather what miserable weeds could be eaten. And although it was very hard work, the children would help their parents in what small ways they could. Yet for all these efforts there was never enough food to solve their hunger.

The youngest of them all, a little frail boy, did not seem fit for any such work. You see, he was quite weak and small, and the people of the village said that he could never grow very big.

And though he was bright and clever, at the end of each day when his brothers and sisters would bring home some precious food, all he would have were empty hands and an embarrassed smile. His parents knew that he could not help the family and worried that this extra burden was unfair to the others, who worked so very hard.

In the end, they decided to take him to the village temple. There, they humbly asked the venerable priest if he would have their son for his acolyte. The old man spoke kindly to the boy and put some hard questions to him. So clever were the child's answers that the priest agreed to let him stay there and promised to teach him all that a priest should know.

Then, as the boy stood with the priest, his parents bowed in thanks and set off to go back to the farm. But his mother turned back because she was his mother and could not leave without hugging him and stroking his hair once more. Then, looking closely at her son, she spoke.

"Do not forget," she said to him, "avoid large places at night; keep to small."

With that she turned, and with quick steps, caught up to her husband on the road that led away from the temple and back to their farm.

The boy did not understand what his mother's words to him had meant, and although he thought and thought about them as he undid his small bundle, he still could not decipher their meaning.

The boy quickly learned what the old priest patiently taught him, and he was very obedient in most things. But he had an odd habit—a fault, the priest said. You see, he drew cats—even where cats ought not to have been drawn. He drew them on the margin of the priest's book, he drew them on the screens in the temple, on the pillars.

More than once the priest told him this was not right, that the cats did not belong in the temple—and more than once the boy sincerely apologized for his efforts. But soon again, there they would be: more pictures of cats, very clever pictures to be sure, but alas, quite inappropriate.

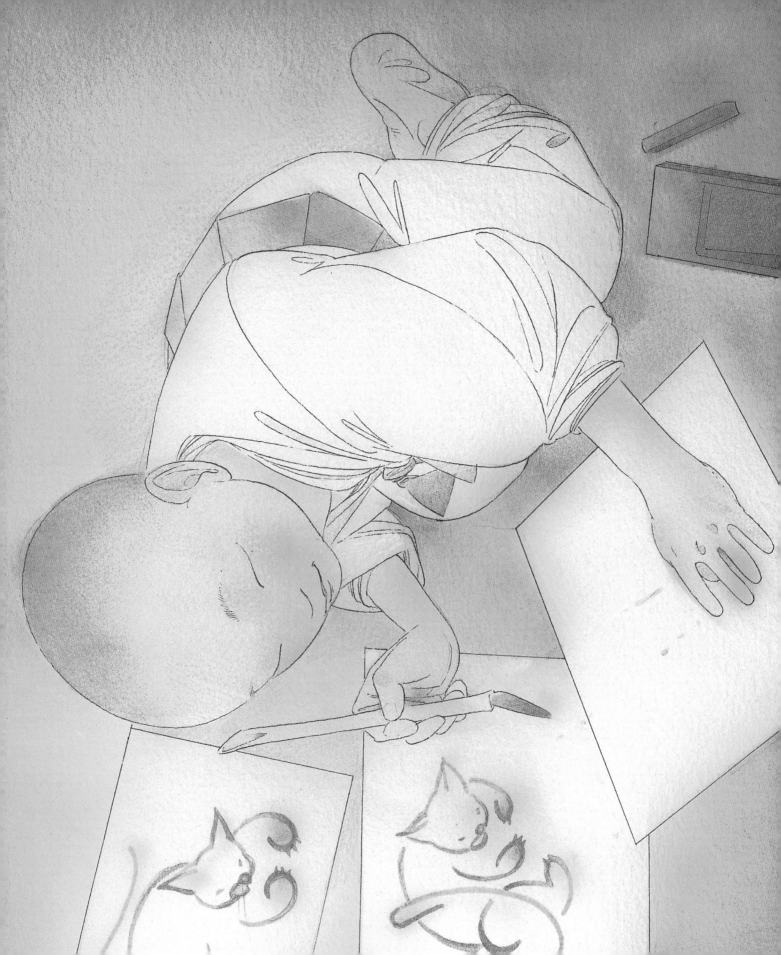

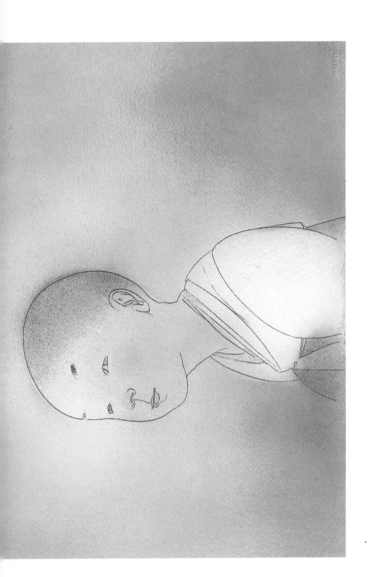

Zow, ever since the demon had come, life had been very hard. Everyone in the region had suffered as the farmer and his family had suffered, and neither the bravest among them, nor the strongest, had been able to deliver them from the famine.

At last, the priest made a pronouncement to all the village. He declared that in order to rid them of the plague, he himself would take on the demon. He would copy out the mystical sutra one thousand times—the ultimate spiritual magic.

He carefully ground some ink in his stone and dipped his brush and began to copy out the most sacred text—once, ten times, twenty-five times. He bent over his work hour after hour. When he had written it nearly two hundred times he set down his brush and sat back, exhausted. Rubbing his eyes, he noticed the boy, his new acolyte, watching him.

"Here now," he said, indicating the scroll, "you are clever, aren't you? Your soul is nearly as earnest as mine. Perhaps you can copy for a while."

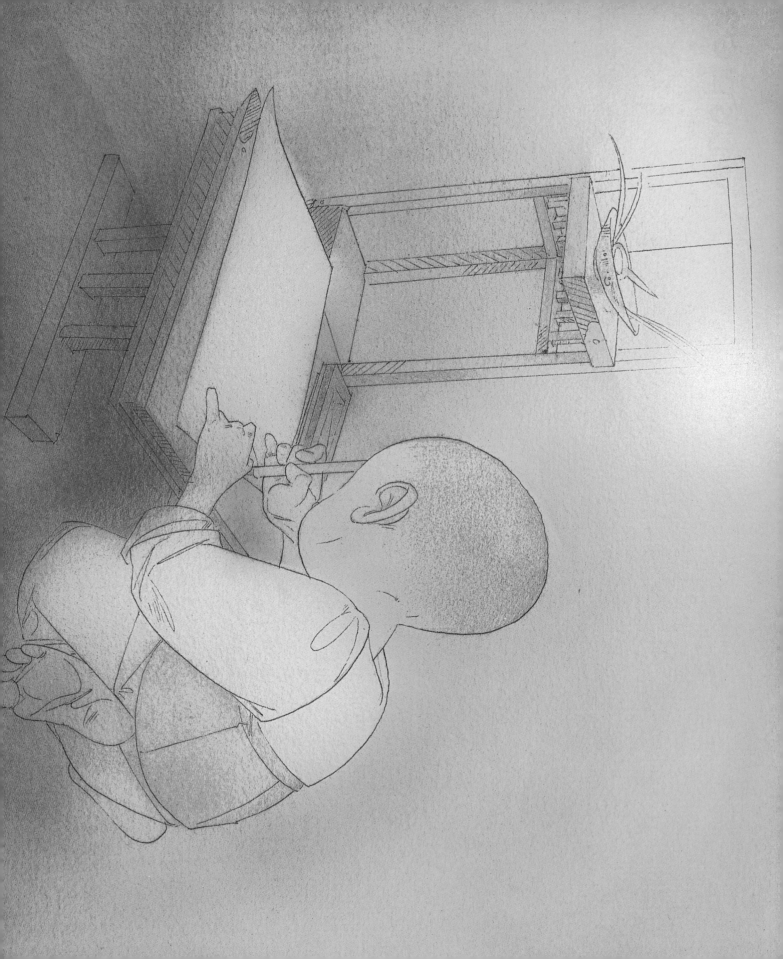

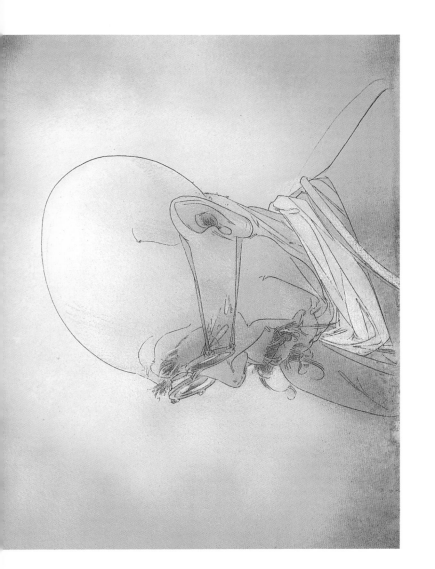

The boy copied well—neatly and with a steady hand. He thought that perhaps by doing this he could help his family, and he happily applied himself to the task. But it was a tedious task to be sure.

That evening the priest returned and, seeing the completed work, he smiled.

On examining the manuscript more closely, though, the priest's smile turned to a frown.

He held the paper out for the boy to see. There, and there, and there. Cats. In the margins, between the characters. There were no cats in the lotus sutra. The priest closed his eyes tightly with anger and then tore up the manuscript.

"It simply won't do," he said. "You can stay here no longer. You must leave in the morning."

With that the priest left, shaking his head and wringing his hands.

The young boy was left alone, dishonored and ashamed. He collected his ink and brush and few things and ordered them so as not to disturb the priest in the morning.

It was only then, in this moment of shame that his mother's words came back to him: "Avoid large places at night; keep to small." So he looked in all the corners of the temple, under the steps, and behind the screens, until, at last, he found a small box with curious hinges and carved handles. He squeezed inside it, and no sooner than he had closed the top over himself, he fell fast asleep.

When he awoke he wished that he could stay there curled up in the box forever. Even so, he knew that he must leave. He lifted open the top of his cabinet, crawled out, drew up his small bundle, and turned to face the grey dawn.

But as he looked around him he gasped. The temple! It had been nearly destroyed! The screens were torn, the floors were splintered, the idols had been shattered.

And there, in the middle of the floor, sat the venerable priest. His robes were in shreds and his body was disfigured with bruises and cuts. He scarcely moved. He lifted his head painfully and looked at the boy with burning eyes.

"The demon," he whispered through cracked and swollen lips. "You must go away at once. Your foolishness has brought evil to this temple."

Then, closing his eyes, the priest let his head drop back down, consumed by his own misfortune.

The boy left the temple, and burdened with guilt for the great destruction his behavior had caused, he set off on the road away from the village.

He walked all morning until, with the sun high in the sky, he came into a small hamlet. He saw only a few simple houses, but they were all quiet and closed and empty seeming, except the very last. The boy approached the threshold and looked.

A man, a very blacksmith, crouched beside his forge, at work on some foundry. Suddenly he sat upright and turned around.

"The demon has chased them all away. Every one of them. Now I am left here alone. But I will not be afraid. As you can see."

He held up an iron bar.

"I am forging a deadly sword. To kill the goblin!"

He swung it with a trenchant stroke.

"You have come here to help me? Of course! Though you do not seem over burly."

He pinched the boy's thin arm.

"Still, you should be fit to work the bellows."

The boy, with his native curiosity and eagerness to serve, was soon adept at this labor, which did not take strength as much as regularity and persistence. Satisfied with his young apprentice, the smith took off his apron.

"I must fetch water to quench the iron and temper the blade. The well is some distance. I will try not to be long, but you must keep the fire going. Just be diligent and I shall return shortly."

The bellows wheezed regularly, firing the coals. And as the boy stared at the glowing embers, all manner of odd shapes came to life before him— birds, houses, faces—and cats. Yes, cats. Scattered untidily about him on the ground were scraps of black charcoal from the forge. He picked one up and tried it on the wall. Indeed, it made a clear, black line—which became a long tail—which became a large, crouching cat....

By the time the smith returned, there were dozens of cats. The boy heard his cough at the door and was suddenly recalled to himself. They both turned to the forge. The bellows lay still; the coals had cooled; and the metal was cold and black.

utting down the bucket, the smith looked about and laughed.

"Ho, ho. You will never be a smith, my boy, that is certain."

The boy hung his head in remorse.

"The cats are fine cats, mind you, but I'm afraid they won't do here."

The smith picked up a straw brush.

"As long as I have brought all this water . . ."

He handed the brush to the boy.

"I would be grateful if you scrubbed them away." When the cats were gone, the smith shared his rice and told the boy he could spend the night there in the shop, if he liked. The smith then retired to his own room in the back and went to sleep.

The boy again found himself alone, and, as before, he recalled his mother's words: "Avoid large places; keep to small." Discovering a large kettle, he squeezed into it, drew on the lid and, tired from the day's journey, he quickly fell to sleep.

ate in the night he woke with a start. His eyes were stinging and it was hard to breathe. Peering out from his hiding place he saw that the blacksmith's shop was on fire! He quickly climbed out of his pot and ran into the street. There he found the smith: his clothes were charred and torn and smoking; his face was blackened; his hair was singed.

At length the smith stuttered, "The demon— the devil—the beast!" He then turned and walked off into the morning mist.

Again the boy felt downcast, thinking that somehow this would not have happened had he only been more diligent, but now he could do nothing.

He started out again on the road away from his home.

It was dusk already and he had seen neither a soul nor a human dwelling all day.

Then, suddenly, a village appeared in front of him. Perhaps he had fallen asleep as he walked. There was no sign of any inhabitant; the houses and shops were closed and dark.

As he looked around, he noticed that everything was grey with dust and thickly spun over with cobwebs. He wiped at the dust with his fingers. Then, in the streaks his fingers left behind, he saw them—the whiskers of another cat. The boy squinted at this drawing, smiled, and drew his painting box out from his bundle.

B ut then, at the far end of the street—on a hill—he saw a large building, perhaps a temple. And faintly flickering inside, he saw a light.

At once the boy went up to the building and knocked; and knocked again; and yet once more, but still nobody came. At last he pushed gently at the door and was pleased to find that it had not been fastened. So he went in and saw a lamp burning. But there was no one there.

It was very very late at night and the boy was very, very tired. But there were cats on all the walls, cats on the screens, cats on the pillars, crouching and sleeping and pouncing—and cats just sitting and watching. Every kind of cat and cats doing everything a cat would do the boy had drawn.

He began to nod asleep, when suddenly he remembered his mother's words, just as though she were whispering in his ear: "Avoid large places at night; keep to small."

And although he could not quite understand them, as he thought of these words now, he felt for the first time a little afraid. The building was very large and the boy was all alone. In one corner, almost hidden with dust, there stood a rickety little cabinet, with a sliding door. He crept into it, slid the door to, shut his eyes and fell instantly asleep.

ery, very late, he was awakened by a most terrible noise! Fighting, screaming, crying, and howling. Here, then there, then there. Then it was all around him, very close by—then it was suddenly far away.

Scraping and scratching and screaming. Awful and then more awful and then more awful yet, so that the building itself rocked. The boy hoped

that the end would come quickly or he should die of very fright. He lay there in the cabinet, perfectly still. And after a long time, silence came. But he was yet afraid to leave his secret shelter.

He did not move until the light of the morning sun shone through the cracks in the cabinet, and he could faintly hear the sounds of the birds heralding the day.

Only then did he very cautiously slide open the door of his hiding place, and look about. The first thing that he saw was the floor, red with blood. And then, lying quite dead in the middle of it, he beheld an enormous, monstrous rat— a demon rat—a rat bigger even than a cow.

But who or what could have killed it? There was no man or other creature to be seen.

Then, the boy saw the mouths and paws of all the cats that he had drawn the night before.

They were red; they were wet with blood. He stood staring at his cats all around him for a very long time. Then, when the sun was high in the sky, he left the temple and started down the road towards his village.

The boy continued to draw cats, and after a time, he became a very great artist. It is said that some of the cats he drew are still shown to travelers in Japan today.

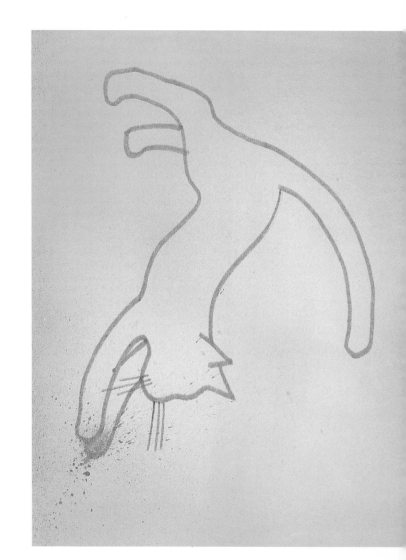